First published in German as *Ein Wintermärchen* by Rotapfel Verlag, Erlenbach-Zürich in 1924. First published by Floris Books, Edinburgh in 2017. This second edition 2022. © 2016 NordSüd Verlag AG. English version © 2017, 2022 Floris Books. All rights reserved
British Library CIP Data available  ISBN 978-178250-818-2  Printed in China through Imago

Printed on sustainably
sourced FSC® paper.
Uses plant-based inks,
which reduces
chemical emissions.

FSC
www.fsc.org

MIX
Paper | Supporting
responsible forestry
FSC® C005748

**Carbon neutral**
Print product
ClimatePartner.com/15859-2204-1001

# The Gnomes' Winter Journey

*Ernst Kreidolf*

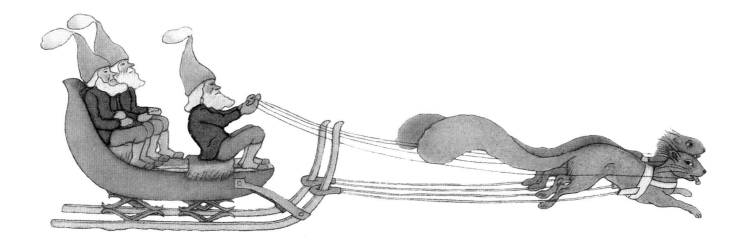

Floris
Books

The first snowstorm of winter swept in, frosting the forest in glittering white. Most of the woodland creatures were safely tucked up in their cosy homes, but three excited forest gnomes were watching the sky.

"The Winter Queen promised she would arrive with the first snow this year," said Grandfather Gnome.

"I think I can see her!" shouted Young Gnome.

"She's heading towards the mountain gnomes' cave!" exclaimed Father Gnome. "Let's visit our cousins for the Winter Queen's welcome feast."

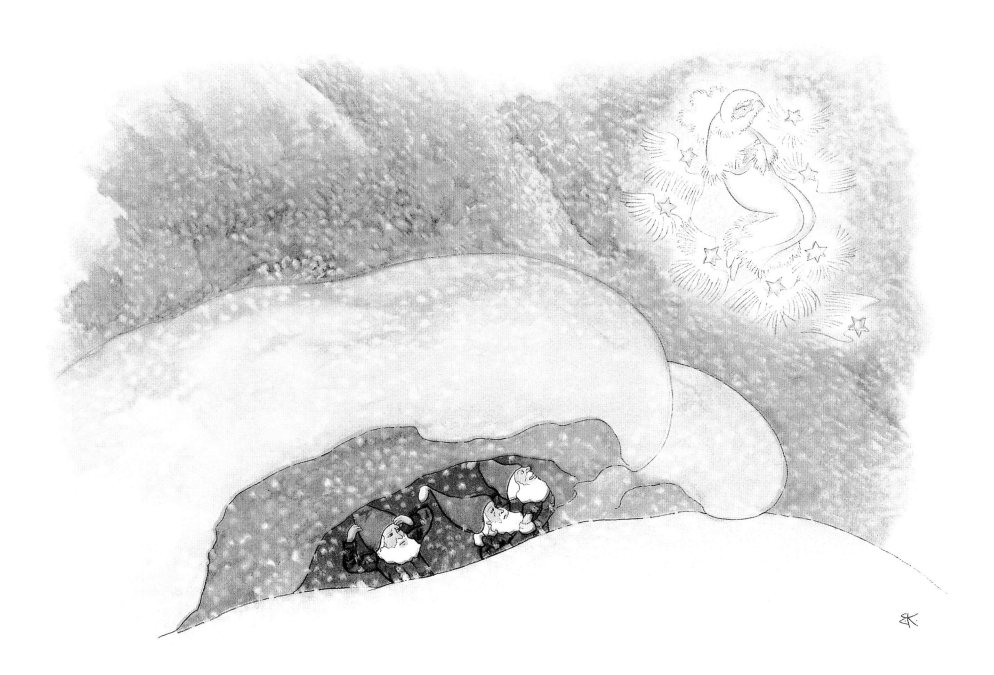

As soon as the snowstorm had passed, the gnomes began their journey.

They'd not gone far when Grandfather Gnome spotted a flock of bright bullfinches and stopped to watch them. The hungry birds were pecking at frozen berries high up in the rowan trees. Beautiful birdsong filled the air.

"The Winter Queen would love to hear these bullfinches singing," sighed Young Gnome.

"We'll see the Winter Queen soon enough," said Father Gnome. "But we must hurry so we aren't late for the feast."

As the gnomes trekked further into the forest, the snow grew deeper and deeper. They found strong sticks to help them wade through the drifts.

Above them, the darkening sky cast strange shadows among the trees. Young Gnome glanced around. "I can see dogs and dragons, elephants and giant birds, crocodiles and… monsters!" he squeaked.

"Hush now, they're only shapes in the snow," reassured Grandfather Gnome.

They hiked on quietly, until they found a sheltered spot to spend the night.

The next morning the gnomes woke before sunrise and continued on their journey. But all they could see was snow, and before long they were lost.

"How will we find our way to the Winter Queen's feast?" said Father Gnome.

"Look!" Young Gnome pointed ahead. "I can see something fluttering over there."

The gnomes made their way to a frozen pond where three snow fairies were ice-dancing in the dawn light. The gnomes stayed hidden for a while, mesmerised by the graceful dancers, until Grandfather Gnome decided, "We should ask these fairies the way."

The three gnomes popped up from behind a snowdrift, and the snow fairies immediately stopped dancing.

"We didn't mean to frighten you. We're lost," said Grandfather Gnome softly. "Can you tell us the way to the home of the mountain gnomes?"

The snow fairies didn't utter a word – they were much too shy. But as they hurried off, one turned back and gestured which way to go.

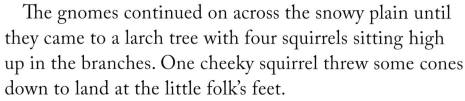

The gnomes continued on across the snowy plain until they came to a larch tree with four squirrels sitting high up in the branches. One cheeky squirrel threw some cones down to land at the little folk's feet.

"You little rascals," Young Gnome called and threw a snowball back at the squirrels.

Soon they were all laughing as cones and snowballs flew back and forth between them.

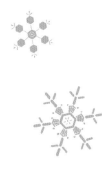

When they were out of breath, Father Gnome asked, "Do you know the way to the home of the mountain gnomes? We're going there to welcome the Winter Queen."

"It will take a long time," one squirrel replied. "You need a sledge – and we can help you!"

The squirrels scurried away and brought back a shining sledge. "Jump on," they cried. And off they all sped, up hills and down valleys, gliding over the snow.

Just as the sun began to set, the sledge slowed.

"Here we are," announced the squirrels. The gnomes jumped down.

"Thank you for the ride, kind squirrels!" The gnomes waved as they watched their new friends head back home.

They tiptoed past a sleeping ice gnome, heading towards the entrance to the mountain gnomes' cave.

"Look at those tall icicles," said Young Gnome.

"I bet you can't climb one," said Grandfather Gnome mischievously.

"I bet we can!" said the other two, and they all clambered up.

As they got higher they heard a loud snap and one of the icicles broke off, sending Young Gnome tumbling to the ground! He sprung up, laughing, as the other two climbed down.

But their game had woken the ice gnome, who shook his head and asked sternly, "I suppose you have come to see the Winter Queen?"

"Yes, we have. Could you please let us in?" Father Gnome asked politely.

"Follow me." The ice gnome's frozen joints cracked as he walked into the cave.

The ice gnome led them through a long dark tunnel to a clearing in the forest, where stars were already twinkling in the clear night sky.

The mountain gnomes were sitting around a large tree, which was completely hidden by snow, enjoying the warmth of a roaring fire. They called out, "Welcome, cousins!" as the forest gnomes hurried over to greet them.

"The Winter Queen has arrived and you're just in time for the feast," said one mountain gnome. They shared news around the warm fire until the bell rang for dinner.

The little folk rushed into the dining hall, where the Winter Queen was waiting for them.

"My dear gnomes," she said, "thank you for welcoming me. I am so happy to see you all again, and to give you my blessing for the winter ahead."

"Dear Winter Queen," the oldest mountain gnome replied, "we are honoured to have you with us and we hope you enjoy your stay. Now, let the feast begin!"

The excited gnomes chatted while they ate delicious pies and cakes that the ice gnome had made.

On the stroke of midnight the mountain gnomes led their guests outside to a glittering frozen pond.

The stars twinkled as two gnomes tapped gently on dangling icicles, sending an enchanting melody through the air.

The Winter Queen, and her friends the snow fairies, moved gracefully over the ice, welcoming the winter with a swirling dance.

The other little folk watched, and when the performance finished they burst into wild applause.

But it was late and, tired after their long journey, the forest gnomes reluctantly went to bed.

The next day the forest gnomes woke to a dazzling view, with pure white snow as far as the eye could see.

"A perfect day for winter games!" said Father Gnome excitedly, and they all headed out to play.

The first game was sledging. The forest gnomes each took a sledge and raced the mountain gnomes' toboggan down a slippery hill. The Winter Queen was the judge.

The mountain gnomes were ahead all the way, but their cheeky forest cousins still shouted, "Winter Queen, Winter Queen, have we won?"

"I'm afraid not," she laughed. "Maybe next time."

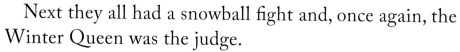

Next they all had a snowball fight and, once again, the Winter Queen was the judge.

There were many more mountain gnomes than forest gnomes, so the hosts were favourites to win. But their cousins were quick on their feet and kept hitting their targets: on the head, on the back – even on the nose!

"The forest gnomes have won!" the Winter Queen declared.

"All that practice with the squirrels must have helped," chuckled Young Gnome.

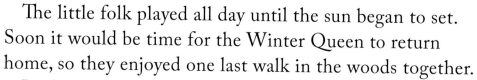

The little folk played all day until the sun began to set.
Soon it would be time for the Winter Queen to return
home, so they enjoyed one last walk in the woods together.

In the frozen forest the branches glistened with frost
and ice. One mischievous gnome climbed high and shook
a shower of ice crystals over his friends.

"How cheeky you all are!" laughed the Winter Queen.
"I'll miss your jokes and games."

Too soon, it was time for the Winter Queen to say goodbye.

"Thank you for such a wonderful time," she called as a whirlwind of snow lifted her up into the sunset and carried her away.

"Goodbye, Winter Queen!" cried the little folk. "See you next year!"

After the Queen had gone, it was the forest gnomes' turn to say goodbye. "Thank you for your kindness, cousins. We must be on our way." And they strapped on the skis they'd borrowed and turned to leave.

"We'll visit you in the summertime," the mountain gnomes shouted after them.

The little folk waved fondly to each other until the forest gnomes disappeared from view, on the long journey home.

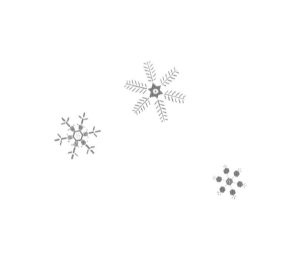